W9-CEM-875

WINNING SEASON

TAKING CONTROL OF THE GAME . . .

The Grotto players had come close to scoring, but they'd also made a key mistake. Every blue shirt except the goalie and one defender was on this end of the field. Calvin booted the ball toward Angel near the sideline, then went full speed up the field. Angel had lots of room and dribbled past Coach Diaz, across the center line, and well into the Grotto side. He passed to Zero, who passed to Orlando, who passed over to Calvin at the top of the penalty area.

It was just Calvin and the goalie now, and Calvin was up to the task. He dribbled straight into the goal box, made a quick feint to his left, then drove the ball hard into the net. Little Italy had the lead.

"Defense now!" Calvin shouted as he ran back into position.

Little Italy tightened its zone, hustled for every loose ball, and held its ground. When the final whistle blew, Calvin dropped to his knees and raised his fists.

"You're the man!" shouted Zero, putting his hands on Calvin's shoulders and squeezing.

Calvin was exhausted but thrilled. He yanked off his T-shirt and wiped his face and shoulders, then walked proudly off the field.

WINNING SEASON

RICH WALLACE

SCHOLASTIC INC.

New York Toronto London Auckland Sydney
Mexico City New Delhi Hong Kong Buenos Aires

For Ryan and Heather

ISBN 0-439-89903-6

 Published by Scholastic Inc., 557 Broadway, New York, NY 10012, by arrangement with Puffin Books, a member of Penguin Group (USA) Inc.

12 11 10 9 8 7 6 5 4 3 2 1 6 7 8 9 10 11/0

Printed in the U.S.A. 40

First Scholastic printing, September 2006

Book design by Jim Hoover
Set in Caslon 224 Book

ALSO BY RICH WALLACE

Winning Season Series

Fast Company

The Roar of the Crowd

Technical Foul

Losing Is Not an Option

Playing Without the Ball

Restless: A Ghost's Story

Shots on Goal

Wrestling Sturbridge

• CONTENTS •

1

The Pizza Division

Calvin Tait stepped outside, walked across the short front lawn, and immediately started sweating. *Another brutal day,* he thought. *Must be ninety already.*

Gazing down the hill and way across the Hudson River, he could see the New York City skyline, shining in the sun but dimmed by the early summer haze. He made his way up the walk of the neighboring house and rapped on the door.

Zero answered within seconds, yanking the door open. "Yo," he said.

Calvin pushed past Zero into the house. "You got the air on?"

"Nah. My dad said not to."

"Not until it breaks a hundred, huh?"

"Something like that," Zero said. "Anyway, we're going out, right?"

"Yeah. We need to get downtown and check out the rosters. Practice starts *tonight,* man. I can't wait."

"I just gotta get some socks. Come on."

Calvin followed Zero up the stairs, winding past an overflowing laundry basket, a stack of news magazines, Zero's black leather sneakers, and a fat orange cat that lifted its tail and mewed.

Zero yanked open a drawer in his small wooden dresser and grabbed an armload of socks. "Need to find a matching pair," he said, dumping the socks onto the bed.

"They're *all* white," Calvin said. "They're bleached whiter than you are."

"Yeah, but they're different." Zero picked up three of the socks. "This one's got a yellow stripe along the top edge. This other one's got thin little ribs. This one has thicker ribs and a gray heel."

"You gotta be kidding me."

"Just give me a second." Zero kept pawing through the pile of socks until he found a pair.

Calvin rolled his eyes. "You could try sorting

them out *before* you dump ’em in the drawer.”

Zero frowned but gave it some thought. “That sounds a little compulsive, don’t you think?”

They went downstairs and Calvin took a seat at the dining-room table. Zero put on his socks, then went back up the stairs to get his sneakers. Calvin reached across and examined the large plastic chicken that sat in the place of honor at the center of the table.

“Don’t mess with that,” Zero said, running down the stairs.

“Just looking.”

“That thing’s fifty years old, at least. My great-grandmother brought it over when she immigrated from Brooklyn.”

“It’s an imitation chicken,” Calvin said.

“It’s an *heirloom,* dude.”

“It’s plastic.”

“Yeah. It’ll last forever.”

Calvin stared at the chicken. Parts of the brown plastic were painted, so the head was red, the tail feathers were black, and the feet were yellow. Some of the paint was peeling away.

“It’s old. I don’t doubt that,” Calvin said.

"It's valuable," Zero said. "Believe me."

Zero finished tying his shoes. "So what are we doing again?" he asked.

"We need to get to the Y and check out the teams."

They had signed up for the YMCA's summer soccer league for eleven- and twelve-year-olds. Both of them had a lot of sports experience—football, basketball, baseball, track. Neither had played much soccer before, but the summer league was a big deal in this town. Coaches from the Hudson City Soccer Club and the St. Joseph's parish squad watched the league closely to recruit new talent for their fall squads.

"Hope we get on the same team," Calvin said.

"We should. My mom told them we had to be together for carpooling to practices and games."

Calvin laughed. "Right. The next time we get a ride anywhere will be the first."

They walked downtown past blocks of tightly packed houses. At the corner of Fifth Street they turned onto the Boulevard and stopped to look in Amazing Ray's 99-Cent Store, the windows stacked with rolls of paper towels and laundry detergent and cases of Goya pineapple drink.

The YMCA was an old brick building on the Boulevard near St. Joseph's Church. It had no pool, but the small gymnasium got plenty of use—basketball, floor hockey, gymnastics.

"Hello, boys," said the woman at the front desk.

"Hi," said Calvin. "Have they posted the teams for the soccer league yet?"

"Right in the gym."

"Thanks."

They entered the gym and started scanning the rosters on the bulletin board.

"Check it out," Zero said, pointing to one of the lists. "We're in the pizza division."

Calvin saw their names under Little Italy, the sponsoring business. There were nine or ten players listed for each team. Because the rec field was small, games in this league were played with just seven players from each team on the field.

LITTLE ITALY

Victor Alvarez

Julie Carrasco

Orlando Green

Peter Leung

Angel Medina
Mary Pineda
Zach "Zero" Rollison
Calvin Tait
Briana Torres

"Little Italy?" Calvin said. "Looks more like Little Cuba; you're the only white kid on the team. Anyway, I heard the winner of the pizza division has won the league like four out of the past five years." He studied the lists again.

EASTERN DIVISION
Villa Roma
Luigi's
The Grotto
Little Italy

WESTERN DIVISION
Hudson City Florist
Bug Busters Extermination
Hector's Garage
Bauer Electric

Each team would play the others in its division twice and the teams in the opposite division once, for a total of ten games. The first two in each division would make the playoffs.

"Do we get free pizza after the games?" Zero asked.

"Doubt it," Calvin said. "Maybe if we win the championship."

"Not *if*," Zero said. "You mean *when* we win it. Think positive, man. Like me."

They left the Y and started walking along the Boulevard. It was eleven A.M. in the middle of June. There'd be a practice session tonight at six thirty. Until then, they had nothing really to do.

2

Leeches

Getting to Hamilton Park from the Hudson City business district requires a steep downhill walk along a rutted old sidewalk. Down here by the waterfront, you cross Palisades Avenue and the park stretches out in front of you for about a hundred yards to the Hudson River and about five hundred yards along it. Directly across in Manhattan are the piers with the giant container ships.

Calvin had a twenty-ounce bottle of lemon-flavored water and had tied his white T-shirt around his waist. Streams of sweat were running from his hair down his dark brown face. He could taste it at the corners of his mouth. "Let's get to the river," he said to Zero. "I'm going in. I don't care who arrests me."

"Nobody's gonna arrest us," Zero said. "Just might get a skin disease from the water."

"I got tough skin."

They crossed the jogging/biking/Rollerblading path that circled the park and stepped onto the large, flat, grassy area in the middle. A man was throwing a Frisbee to his dog, and a few other people in the park were sitting on benches or sprawled out under the maple trees, hoping to catch a breeze from the water.

But what caught Calvin's eye was a group of six teenagers on the far side of the park, energetically kicking a soccer ball in a three-on-three match and shouting in Spanish. The player with the ball was laughing as two frustrated opponents tried to steal it. He bobbed around them and kept the ball amazingly close to his feet, starting and stopping and then bursting between them and passing to a wide-open teammate.

"Cool," Calvin said.

Zero shook his head and wiped his forehead with the back of his hand. "Hot."

Calvin rolled his eyes. "I mean his *moves.* That's good soccer."

The boys reached the railing above the river. The tide was low, so there was a few feet of muddy bank between the river and the retaining wall. They could easily hop over the fence and wade.

Calvin tossed his shirt and the water bottle onto the grass and said, "Let's go." In one fluid motion he was over the fence, down the wall, and onto the bank.

Zero quickly followed. "Don't take your shoes off," he said.

"What am I, stupid?" Calvin walked knee-deep into the water. He reached down and cupped some into his hands, soaking his skinny chest and shoulders. "Feels good," he said.

"Things better cool off before practice tonight," Zero said.

"Maybe a degree or two."

"Never thought I'd be playing soccer."

"You know what my dad wanted me to do instead?" Calvin asked. "Take *golf* lessons. Golf! He took me to one of those pitch-and-putt courses out by Livingston a couple of weeks ago. Par fifty-four. It took me a *hundred* and fifty-four."

"Not your sport, huh?"

"Maybe later in life. Like retirement age."

A wadded-up piece of paper hit Calvin in the shoulder and he quickly turned around. Twin black-haired girls his age were standing on the path, leaning over the railing and grinning. Jessie and Danielle Rosado. Both girls were lean and witty. Calvin knew them well.

Calvin scooped up the paper and hurled it back. "Don't pollute, ladies," he said.

"Heard you boys are playing soccer," said Jessie, the twin with wild braids.

"You heard right," said Calvin.

"What team you on?" asked Danielle, who'd had her hair straightened.

"Little Italy," said Zero. "You playing?"

"Of course," said Jessie. "Bauer Electric. We got second in the whole league last year and we have seven players back. This year we're gonna win it."

"We'll see about that," said Calvin.

"We're the *electric* team," said Danielle. "We'll shock you."

"We'll light you up," added Jessie, laughing.

"Oh yeah?" said Zero. "Well, we'll . . . we'll pizza you."

"Good one, Z," said Calvin.

The girls looked at each other and rolled their eyes. They started walking away. Jessie looked back and said to Calvin, "Watch out for leeches."

"There ain't no leeches in here," Calvin said, but he pulled one leg from the water and looked at it. "The mercury kills 'em."

"There's leeches everywhere," said Jessie. "Beware."

Zero stepped into the water, then turned and watched the twins walk away. "There's girls in this league?" he said to Calvin.

"Didn't you look at the rosters? We got three girls on our own team."

"Oh, yeah." Zero nodded his head and a slow smile started to creep across his face. "Guess that's not so bad," he said.

Calvin grinned. "Not so bad," he said, pointing toward the Rosados, who were fifty yards away by now. "Not so bad at all."

3

Toasted

The YMCA league started with a full-league clinic, where the basics of passing, dribbling, shooting, goaltending, and defense were taught. The players broke into several groups for the drills.

Calvin was a natural athlete, quickly picking up any game he tried. But within minutes of the start of the clinic he realized that he had some work to do if he was going to excel in this league. He could handle the ball all right, but he was continually faked out by more experienced players.

Here was Jessie Rosado during a one-on-one drill, stepping left then quickly going right, guiding the ball with the outside of her foot as Calvin lunged in the wrong direction.

Then came Johnny Rodriguez, deftly stepping over the ball, tapping it with his heel, and leaving Calvin flat-footed as he darted toward the goal.

"Watch the ball, Calvin, not the player," said Luis Diaz, the teenager whose rapid footwork Calvin had admired in the park that afternoon. Luis was a key player on Hudson City's high-school team and one of the coaches in this summer league. "They can make all the dodges and jukes they want, but if you keep your eyes on the ball, they won't fake you out. You'll catch on. You've got the skills."

Calvin nodded. This wouldn't be easy, but he'd get it.

He did better with dribbling—his excellent speed and coordination were a big plus there. But he needed to work on that as well. "Don't just kick it and chase it," said coach Irvin Cornell, who'd played soccer at Essex Community College. "Touch the ball with every step when you dribble."

Calvin found Zero after the clinic, sitting on the bottom row of the metal bleachers. "That was harder than I expected," he said, wiping his brow with his hand. "There are some *good* players here."

"Did you play goalie at all?" Zero asked. His cheeks were red from exertion.

"Nope. We didn't get to that."

"I was pretty good at it."

Calvin sat down and took off his cleats. He put on his sneakers and a dry T-shirt. "Gotta get shin guards," he said.

"I know."

The Rosado twins had walked over. "Hey, Calvin," said Jessie.

"What's up?"

"I smoked you, dude." She was smiling.

Calvin tried to look unimpressed. "Once."

"It's that electricity we told you about."

Zero elbowed Calvin and raised his eyebrows.

Jessie went through the motions of the fake, leaning to her left then darting sideways to her right. "One little move and he was toast," she said.

"The truth?" asked Zero.

Calvin shrugged and gave an embarrassed grin. "Guess so."

"Well, there's our ride," said Jessie, pointing toward a station wagon that was pulling into the parking lot. She winked at Calvin. "Hope I don't give you nightmares. See you next time."

Danielle waved to the boys with her fingers and followed Jessie across the field.

Calvin stared after them, resting his chin on his fist. Then he caught Zero's eye and gently shook his head a few times, breaking into a smile. "I'm starving," he said. "You got money?"

"Yeah. You?"

"Yeah. Not a lot."

"Enough?"

"Yeah. Enough for something. Let's go."

Calvin gathered up his cleats, the soaking-wet T-shirt, and a plastic gallon jug that he'd filled with water. He'd finished half of it during breaks. "Shoulda brought a gym bag," he said.

"Where we going?"

"The market, I guess."

They headed toward the small grocery store at the corner of Ninth and the Boulevard. Hudson City's main street was busy with traffic, and many of the shops and small restaurants were open late on summer evenings. Music was coming from many of the stores, which occupied the bottom floors of the two- and three-story buildings.

It was about eight twenty when the boys reached the grocery.

"What do we want?" Zero asked.

Calvin squinted and looked around the store, nodding thoughtfully. "I'm narrowing it down," he said. "Something substantial . . . maybe from the deli."

They headed down the canned-goods and juice aisle and made a left toward the deli counter. There were no other customers so they didn't bother taking a number.

"Help you?" asked the bored teenage boy behind the counter.

"In due time," said Calvin, peering into the glass case at the cold cuts and tubs of salads. "The fruit salad looks good. Roast beef . . . salami." He tapped on the glass. "That potato salad fresh?" he asked.

"Wouldn't be in there if it wasn't," the teenager said flatly.

"Let's have half a pound of that with two forks," Calvin said.

The guy dished up the salad and weighed it. "Just over half," he said.

"That'll do us," Calvin said. He looked at Zero. "What else?"

"I was thinking pretzels."

"Excellent choice. And orange juice?"

"Absolutely," Zero said. "Potato salad, pretzels, and orange juice. What could be better?"

"The only thing that could make it better is to eat it all at a bus stop," Calvin said. "Boulevard and Eleventh is my favorite bench. You?"

"Perfect atmosphere," Zero replied. "Let's do it."

4

Three on Three

Two nights later, Coach Luis Diaz blew his whistle sharply and called his team over. They each had a ball and had been working on controlling it, dribbling in and out of a series of cones.

"That's enough of a warm-up," he said. "Drills are fine, but you learn this game by *playing* it."

Calvin and the others kneeled on the grass and looked up at the coach. He was short and sturdy, with the beginnings of a summer mustache sprouting above his lip. He would be captain of the Hudson City High School team this fall.

"How many of you have actually played this game?" he asked. "On a real team, I mean."

Four or five players raised their hands. Zero asked, "Does gym count?"

The coach smiled and shrugged. "Sort of." He made two quick cutting motions with his hand, dividing the group into three sets of three. "You three stand up," he said, indicating Calvin, Mary Pineda, and Peter Leung. "You're a team."

"Just three of us?" Calvin asked.

"Three is the perfect unit. You'll see."

Coach had set up two portable goals, one in front of a full-sized goal and the other at midfield. "Short field. No goalies," he said. "But no long shots, either. I want to see footwork and passing. Any shot longer than fifteen yards doesn't count."

Coach sent Zero, Julie Carrasco, and Orlando Green onto the field for the game. "The game goes for one goal," Coach said. "Losing team steps off and the third team comes on. We'll switch the teammates around after a while."

He blew his whistle and Calvin took possession of the ball, kicking it ahead and chasing it down. The three opponents converged on him, and Calvin pivoted, kicking the ball to the side and throwing out an elbow.

Julie took possession of the ball and booted it up the field, where Peter caught up to it and sent it flying in the other direction.

Now it was simply a race to the ball, and Calvin got there first. With the three opponents in pursuit, Calvin quickly shot the ball toward the goal. It missed by about four feet and spun out of bounds.

Coach Diaz stood with his arms folded and his mouth tight. He stepped over to the three players who were waiting to get in and started talking quietly to them.

On the field, Calvin chased down a long boot from Orlando and came racing back up the field. He dodged past Zero, then managed to spin between Julie and Orlando, finding himself right in front of a wide-open goal. He easily kicked the ball into the net and threw his fists into the air.

He trotted back to his team's end of the field, laughing.

"Okay," Coach said. "Next team."

Angel Medina, Briana Torres, and Victor Alvarez trotted out. All three were a year younger than Calvin.

"We'll eat these guys up," Calvin said to Mary.

Angel came up the field with the ball, and Calvin and his teammates ran toward him. As they approached, Angel turned and sent the ball back to Briana, who was about fifteen feet to the side and behind him.

"Charge!" yelled Calvin with a broad grin, leading his two teammates toward the ball.

But Briana was quick, barely receiving the ball before she passed it over to Victor. By the time Calvin had turned and headed toward Victor, the ball was already moving back to Angel, who easily took it thirty yards to the goal and fired it in.

Coach blew his whistle. "Calvin," he said with a broad smile. "Tell me what just happened."

"That kid scored."

Coach laughed. "How come?"

"Because he got lucky?"

"You tell me. How lucky does he have to be when nobody's guarding him?"

Calvin shrugged. "I got through three of them when I scored."

"It wasn't easy though, was it?"

"Guess not."

"Look," Coach said. "Remember when I said three was the perfect unit? Think about it. While you were fighting to get through three defenders, your two teammates were as wide open as they could be. You had your head down, thinking only about dribbling and shooting. The way to score goals is to *pass*, my man."

Calvin nodded.

"We need to work hard, but we need to work smart. That's all I told these guys," he said, sweeping his hand toward Angel and his two teammates. "When you three went racing after the ball together, all they had to do was form a triangle and make a few simple passes to pick you apart."

"I get it," Calvin said.

"Okay, let's try it some more. Everybody listen: When a player has the ball in a three-on-three game, he should always have two options for passing. Two teammates, two options. Think of a triangle shape."

Coach patiently corrected mistakes every few minutes after that, explaining how a player could have moved into position for a pass, or how a defender could avoid getting faked out. But mostly he let them play, and gradually they began to catch on.

"We'll be pretty good," Coach said after they'd run some laps at the end. "We've got talent; we just have to use our brains."

Calvin and Zero stopped at Little Italy for a slice of pizza on the way home. On the wall beside the counter were several team pictures from previous Little Italy teams, and a plaque from a few years before when the team had won the YMCA title.

"We'll be up there soon," Calvin said, pointing to the pictures as they were served their slices.

"Are you on our team?" said the man behind the counter.

"Yeah," Zero said. "Just finished practice a few minutes ago."

"Ernie Salinardi," the man said, sticking out his hand for them to shake. "I own this place."

Calvin and Zero shook his hand and gave their names.

"It's our first soccer season," Calvin said.

"Great. The team's looking good, I hope?"

"*Real* good," Calvin said. Then he leaned his

head to one side and thought for a second. "We *will* be, anyway. Still got a lot to learn."

"Learn quick," Ernie said, winking. "Wins are good for business."

"We'll try," Zero said, nodding solemnly.

"I'm just kidding." Ernie wiped the counter with a cloth. "Have fun and learn the game. There's no better game on earth."

"It's a deal," Calvin said.

"I only ask one thing," Ernie said, breaking into a grin. "Don't lose to Luigi's. That's my cousin's place. We'll have a dinner wagered on that game, believe me."

5

Opening Day

Coach Diaz carried a box of orange T-shirts across the rec field. He tossed Calvin a shirt with the YMCA logo and LITTLE ITALY in blue block letters. Calvin scrambled out of his tank top and pulled the new shirt over his head. Number 9.

"First game," Coach Diaz said, gathering the team around him. "Two twenty-four minute halves. We'll keep it simple." He held up a clipboard with a diagram of a soccer field drawn on it. "Let's go over the positions again."

"Two wings," he said, circling the LW and RW he'd written on the diagram. "Front line, left and right. You're mostly on offense, but in a seven-on-seven game like this one, you'll need to hustle back on defense, too. Everybody needs to float—don't be a mile away from the ball. But don't crowd up, either. That's what kills an offense."

Coach circled the letter C between the wings. "The center forward. Key guy. Get in position to score."

Calvin could already feel his T-shirt sticking to his back. It was early evening, but the weather remained hot and humid. It hadn't rained in weeks.

Coach pointed to the two MIDs he had written below the front line. "Midfielders. Support the offense; remember that triangle pattern we tried.

And work your butts off on defense. Keep the ball away from our goal.

"Sweeper. You play behind the midfielders but work *with* them.

"Goalie. Stop the shots. When you have the ball, get it up the field to a teammate. Any questions?"

Calvin put up his hand. "What positions are we playing?"

"I'll get to that. One rule. One major, essential, critical rule: Pass the ball. *Pass* it. Then move into position for a return pass. That's how you move the soccer ball. Dribble if you have space, but don't ever just put your head down and chase it."

Coach looked at his watch. "We've got ten minutes. Grab a ball and dribble two laps around the field, then get back here and I'll give you your positions. Let's hustle."

Calvin picked a ball out of the large mesh bag and dropped it at his feet. Several of his teammates were already dribbling along the sideline, but Calvin was the fastest player on the team. He zipped around the corner flag and behind the goal, working the ball with both feet and keeping it as close as he could. It got away from him as he dribbled around the corner, but he recovered it and sprinted up the sideline, passing Orlando, a taller black kid who was fast, but was struggling with the ball. Calvin smiled when he saw the number 0 on the back of the only player still running ahead of him.

"Save some energy," Zero said as Calvin flew past.

"I got plenty," Calvin replied.

The Grotto players were outfitted in dark blue T-shirts. They were in pairs or groups of three, passing the balls back and forth near the middle of the field. It looked as if they had some good players. Calvin still wasn't sure about his own team. Little Italy had a lot of eleven-year-olds, and a few of them weren't very athletic.

Coach put Calvin at sweeper for the first half, with Zero at goalie.

"We may get shell-shocked back here," Calvin said softly as they jogged onto the field. He was looking toward Little Italy's front line—Victor Alvarez, Peter Leung, and Briana Torres. None of the three was taller than five feet.

"That's what we're here for," Zero said. "Look—keep it close this half, then we'll pound 'em later when we move up on offense."

Calvin's concerns proved to be valid. The Little Italy front-line players seemed confused and hurried, swiping at the ball as soon as it came by, booting it up the field but rarely toward a teammate.

The Grotto had some quick players who put the pressure on and kept it up. Calvin twice cleared the ball away from the front of the goal, and Zero made a couple of saves. But the Grotto's tall, red-haired striker eventually took a nice centering pass from the wing, gave a fake and dribbled around Orlando, then fired the ball into the net as Zero dove in vain.

Coach Diaz called the players over before they lined up for the kickoff.

"We have to establish some offense," he said. "We can't just kick it hard every time the ball comes to us. Make some good *short* passes—just try to get into the rhythm of the game. You can pass *back-wards,* you know.

"Midfielders, call for the ball. That's what I mean by support—let them know where you are. You guys aren't talking at all."

Coach gave a big smile as he sent them onto the field. "I like the effort," he said. "But let's use our brains, too."

Peter took the kickoff and made a short pass toward Briana, who trapped the ball, pivoted, and passed back to midfielder Angel Medina. Angel was short and wiry, with olive skin and close-cropped hair. He dribbled a few steps, then made another short pass, this one about ten yards across the field to Mary.

"Support!" yelled Calvin, who had moved up the field. Mary made a nice grass-cutting pass back to him, and Calvin fielded it and surveyed the situation.

Victor, Mary, and Peter were clumped up about ten yards in front of Calvin. "Spread out!" he said firmly, darting to his right. He had room to dribble, but a couple of Grotto players were closing in.

Calvin saw Angel ahead of him near the sideline and made a crisp pass in his direction. Angel moved toward the ball and trapped it, then put on a burst of speed. Coach Diaz clapped his hands as Angel ran by. "That's the way," he called. "Short passes to move the ball!"

Little Italy didn't come close to scoring the rest of the half, but the competition seemed much more balanced. The Grotto made a couple of runs at the goal, but the defense closed ranks, and Zero made two more saves. At halftime, the score was still only 1–0.

"Much better," Coach said as the players sucked on orange slices and swigged water near the wooden bench. "Keep passing. Keep hustling. We'll put more speed up front this half."

Zero moved up to wing and Calvin to midfield. Coach grabbed the sleeve of Calvin's T-shirt and took him aside as the others ran onto the field. "Be aggressive," he said. "You've got the speed to play the whole field. You need to take control of the game."

Calvin nodded. He appreciated the implication that he could play a less rigid game.

Little Italy came out smoking in the second half. With Julie Carrasco, Zero, and Orlando up front and Calvin controlling the midfield, most of the early action was in the Grotto's defensive end.

The ball went out of bounds near the corner, and Orlando scooped it up for a throw-in. His throw reached Zero's feet, and Zero had room to dribble toward the goal. As the defense closed in, Zero chipped the ball into the air toward the goal box.

Calvin got there first, caught the ball softly on his thigh, and let it drop. He had a clear shot at the net, but the goalie was darting over to that side.

Calvin feinted to his right, then passed the ball across the field, parallel to the goal line and zipping across the grass. Julie was there and the net was wide open. She pounded it home. The game was tied!

Calvin raised his fist and punched at the air, shouting, "Yeah!"

Julie ran over and Calvin caught her in a bear hug. Zero patted her shoulder and they ran toward the center of the field.

Calvin looked toward the sideline. Coach tapped the side of his head. "Smart play!" he shouted.

Past the coach and behind the bench, Calvin caught sight of the Rosado sisters, decked out in their black team T-shirts and passing a ball around. Calvin knew they had the second game of the evening, against Hudson City Florist.

"Let's get another one!" Zero said, dropping back a bit for the kickoff. About seven minutes remained in the game. Plenty of time.

Calvin heard a low rumble of thunder in the

distance, but the sky was mostly clear. He was sweating heavily, but his energy level was high. He wanted to win this one badly.

The ball came to him a few moments later, and he angled upfield toward the sideline. He approached the center line but suddenly he was trapped—two defenders in front of him and one at his side, directly between him and Angel.

Peter Leung was playing sweeper, but he was way back near the goal. Calvin sent a long pass toward him, but he didn't get much pace on the ball. Bad move.

A Grotto player raced toward the ball and got there well ahead of Peter, who was cutting over as quickly as he could. That left the middle of the field open, and that red-haired Grotto player was streaking in by himself. The ball had been passed ahead of him and he was chasing it.

Calvin sprinted down the field and shouted to Peter. "Take the middle! I've got your back."

The redhead had the ball now and there was open space between him and the goal. Mary Pineda, short but limber, was crouched in front of the Little Italy net. She hadn't been tested in the entire second half.

Peter raced toward the ball and offered just enough resistance to take away a pure, dead-on shot. So when the shot came, it was from a slight angle, a low line drive that streaked toward the corner of the net. Mary lunged and got a hand on it. The ball popped into the air but continued toward the goal.

Calvin had reached the goal box and threw himself toward the ball. He nudged it with his forehead and it squirted out of the box, bouncing on the grass and rolling toward the corner.

A Grotto player chased it down and chipped it back toward the goal. Calvin intercepted it and looked up the field. Orange and blue shirts were everywhere.

The Grotto players had come close to scoring, but they'd also made a key mistake. Every blue shirt except the goalie and one defender was on this end of the field. Calvin booted the ball toward Angel near the sideline, then went full speed up the field. Angel had lots of room and dribbled past Coach Diaz, across the center line, and well into the Grotto side. He passed to Zero, who passed to Orlando, who passed over to Calvin at the top of the penalty area.

It was just Calvin and the goalie now, and Calvin

was up to the task. He dribbled straight into the goal box, made a quick feint to his left, then drove the ball hard into the net. Little Italy had the lead.

"Defense now!" Calvin shouted as he ran back into position.

Little Italy tightened its zone, hustled for every loose ball, and held its ground. When the final whistle blew, Calvin dropped to his knees and raised his fists.

"You're the man!" shouted Zero, putting his hands on Calvin's shoulders and squeezing.

Calvin was exhausted but thrilled. He yanked off his T-shirt and wiped his face and shoulders, then walked proudly off the field.

Jessie Rosado jogged by closely as Calvin walked off. "Pretty good," she said, not meeting his eyes.

"Thanks," said Calvin, turning to look. Jessie kept jogging. And Calvin walked right into her sister Danielle.

Danielle stumbled backward but smiled. "Yuck," she said, wiping her hands on her shirt. "Is that sweat?"

"What do you think?" Calvin said, grinning. "I been running for forty-eight minutes."

"You ran good," she said. "But watch us now. You'll learn something."

Coach Diaz called the team over. "Great win. Smart and tough. We'll only get better."

Zero punched Calvin's arm. "What now?" he said.

Calvin shrugged. "I need about a gallon of fluid. Let's get something and come back."

"For what?"

"To watch the second game," Calvin said. "Check out the competition." He squinted and looked at the field, where the Bauer Electric players were warming up. "Let's see how good those twins really are. See what makes them tick."

6

The Count

The Rosado twins were excellent players. They scored two goals apiece and totally controlled the game as Bauer Electric put up a dominating 5–0 victory.

Zero and Calvin sat on the grass with quart bottles of Gatorade. The sky grew darker and there was occasional thunder, but things stayed dry during the game. A cooling breeze blew during the second half. Calvin lay back and looked at the clouds rolling in.

"I'm starving," Zero said as the game ended. "I still think we might get free pizza if we wear our jerseys into Little Italy."

"If I wear this jersey anywhere I'll get thrown out

on the street," Calvin said, looking at the balled-up orange shirt on the ground. "It's got about fifteen pounds of sweat in it."

"Let's get pizza anyway," Zero said. "I got money left."

They walked up to the Boulevard. A large wooden sign had been posted on the lawn of St. Joseph's Church, announcing the parish's annual carnival and street fair. It would run for three evenings in July at the field behind the church.

"Definitely gonna hit that a couple of times," Zero said.

"They got great calzones," Calvin said. "And sausage sandwiches."

"How come you're so skinny when all you do is eat?" Zero asked.

"Quick metabolism. And hey, I run my butt off."

"That you do."

Calvin stopped walking and stared at the sign.

"What?" Zero asked.

"Just thinking about the carnival." Calvin clasped his hands and placed them on top of his head. "Just was thinking that there aren't a lot of . . . you know . . . social opportunities like that in this town."

Zero rolled his eyes but smiled. "Oh, man," he said. "The twins?"

"You know what I'm saying." Calvin pointed at the sign. "Fun. Food. Rides. Think we could pull it off?"

Zero shrugged. "Worth trying, I suppose."

"I'll drop a few hints. Test the water, you know. They're pretty sassy, but I think they might join us. We're fairly sophisticated, aren't we?"

Zero laughed. "That's stretching it, I'd say. But I don't know. I always thought they were out of our league."

"The way I see it, we're in the same league at the moment. Just different divisions."

"That's not what I meant."

"I know what you meant." Calvin frowned. "Don't forget, bro—we're undefeated."

The boys juggled their cleats, shin guards, T-shirts, and slices of pizza as they made their way out of the Little Italy restaurant and onto the sidewalk. Ernie Salinardi had greeted them by name and was thrilled that they'd won. "Best pizza in town," he'd said. "Best team, too, I hope."

They were way uptown, between Third and

Fourth Streets, in an area of the Boulevard that was mostly residential—tall old trees and apartment buildings, some huge clapboarded houses, a couple of small shops, and the pizza place.

Calvin stopped walking as they approached the corner. "The Count," he said.

"What?"

Calvin pointed to a man standing near the bus-stop bench, holding a leash attached to a big German shepherd. The man had fuzzy hair sticking out from an old Yankees cap pulled low on his head, and a dark windbreaker. It was hard to tell his age. Thirty-five? Sixty?

"The Count," Calvin repeated. "You never heard of him?"

"Nope."

"He counts buses."

"You're kidding me."

Calvin looked at Zero in disbelief. "You don't get out much, do you? The guy is *legendary* in this town, man. Ask him what the count is."

"Me?"

"Yeah. Ask him."

Zero shook his head, but he took a couple of

steps toward the man, who was staring intently at the Boulevard, looking up the street and then down.

"Hey!" Zero said loudly. He started to laugh. "What's the count?"

The man turned his head slightly and looked blankly at the boys. "Three up, four down," he said softly.

Zero looked at Calvin.

"Down is that way," Calvin whispered, pointing toward Jersey City, "toward the Holland Tunnel. Up is toward the Lincoln. He comes out here every night and counts buses in each direction until one side reaches five. He's been doing it for years. Never says a word unless you ask him what the count is."

"He crazy?"

"I don't know. My father says he's harmless."

"Homeless?"

"*Harm*less. I think he lives right here." Calvin jutted his thumb toward a shabby brick apartment building.

"Here comes one," Zero said loudly, pointing toward a New Jersey Transit bus coming up the hill from Jersey City. "That'll tie it up."

The heavy rain started as the bus went by. Big

cold drops. Within seconds the ground was soaked and steaming, and the rain was pelting their heads. The drops were hitting so hard that they were bouncing off the pavement.

The boys started running back toward their homes, darting across the Boulevard. The downpour had hit so fast that they had to jump across a torrent at the gutter.

"This is nuts!" Calvin said. "What are we running for? We're already soaked."

"It doesn't rain all month and then we get a hurricane!" Zero said.

They glanced back as they reached Fifth Street. The Count was still standing at the bus stop, ignoring the storm. "He won't leave until one side gets to five," Calvin said.

"He *must* be crazy."

"Yeah," Calvin replied. "He must be."

7

Below Minimum

Little Italy stayed unbeaten over the next week. Calvin scored twice in a rout of Villa Roma and once in a wild 4–4 tie with Luigi's.

He was dog-tired as he lay in bed the morning after the tie, staring at the ceiling. It felt as if he'd sprinted up and down that field a hundred times.

So they'd made it through the pizza-division side of the schedule the first time without a loss. But now they'd play the teams in the other division, starting with Bauer Electric and its perfect 3–0 record.

The bedroom door opened and Calvin's dad was standing there with a grin.

"You're off today?" Calvin said.

"Yes I am. You ready to work?"

Mr. Tait was an assistant principal at a high school in Jersey City. He still had the build of a basketball standout, and was usually dressed in a suit and tie. Though classes had ended for the summer, he was at the school most weekdays, taking care of details. Today he was wearing a red golf shirt and tailored shorts. He held up a list and shook it playfully. "Lots of chores," he said.

Calvin nodded reluctantly. "I hear you."

"Garage door needs to be painted. Got some shrubs to plant along the front of the house. Lawn needs trimming." Mr. Tait glanced at the list and rubbed his chin. "That's probably enough." He looked amused. "For this morning."

Calvin sat up and spun his legs to the floor. It was 7:14 A.M. "Starting early, huh?"

His father winked. "Seize the day." He made an embarrassing little dance move, tightening his arms and thrusting his hips to the side.

Calvin winced. "Very cool, Dad."

Twenty minutes later Calvin was stirring paint in the driveway.

"Don't spill it," Dad said. "Keep it on the drop cloth."

Calvin sighed. "I *know,* Dad. I don't intend to spill any."

"Just reminding you. When you go too fast, you screw up."

"I got it, Dad. You gonna stand there and watch me?"

"No-ho-ho," Mr. Tait said, stretching out the word. "I've got plenty to do myself. I'll check up on you from time to time."

Yeah, Calvin thought as his dad went back into the house. *Like every ten minutes.* He climbed a few rungs of the stepladder and started the job, applying the white paint with a brush. It wasn't a hard job, just tedious around the glass windowpanes. Within an hour he was half done.

Zero had come over by then, eating a peanut-butter sandwich and examining Calvin's work. He had bare feet and his curly hair was in disarray from going to sleep right after washing it.

"Missed a spot," Zero said, pointing toward the edge of a pane.

Calvin frowned and dabbed at the spot with his brush. He had a few specks of paint on his arms and his face.

"You're turning white," Zero said with a laugh.

"Guess I been hanging out with you too much. Your genes are rubbing off on me."

"Think you'll be done soon?"

"No. But it don't matter. He's got me working all day."

"Thought we'd hang out later."

"We'll see." Calvin kept painting as they talked, stopping only to study his work, looking for places he'd missed.

"Carnival's next weekend," Zero said.

"Think I don't know that?"

"We getting anywhere?"

"Ain't tried yet. Figured I'd talk to them after the game."

"After we beat 'em?"

"After *whatever.* You seen them play."

"We can beat them."

Calvin nodded slowly. "We'd better."

The back door opened and Mr. Tait came out. He strolled over and looked at the paint job. "Not bad," he said.

"Morning, Mr. Tait," said Zero.

"Hello, Zachary. Nice day, huh?"

"Perfect."

They stood quietly for a moment, watching Calvin paint. "Well," said Zero. "Think I'll watch some TV. See you later." He walked across his backyard and into his house.

"Ambitious kid," Mr. Tait said quietly, with a big dose of sarcasm.

"He's okay," Calvin said.

"He might mow that lawn of theirs." Mr. Tait motioned toward the Rollisons' tiny yard, which had patches of worn dirt and many high tufts of grass that hadn't been mowed in weeks. In contrast, the Taits' lawn was thick and green and was neatly trimmed at the edges. "You can do ours when you finish here."

Calvin was nearly done painting when his mom came out of the house with his four-year-old sister, Chelsea. "Great job!" Mom said. "Look at the work your big man of a brother did, sweetie. Isn't that wonderful?"

Chelsea smiled at Calvin. "You got white freckles," she said.

"We're going food shopping," Mom said. "Anything special you want for dinner?"

"Nah, but could you bring me a drink or something? Dad's gonna have me working all day."

"I'll rescue you," Mom said. "Work until lunchtime. I'll keep your father off your back."

After cleaning up the paint job, Calvin mowed the lawn, which didn't take very long. The lots in this neighborhood were small.

"Three and a half hours' work?" Mr. Tait said as they sat at the kitchen table eating lunch. He opened his wallet and handed Calvin a ten-dollar bill.

Calvin smiled but said, "Don't I get minimum wage, at least?"

"Not in this house, bud."

"Thanks anyway." He folded the bill in half and put it in his pocket.

"You should save some of that," Dad said.

"We'll see."

Calvin went next door and got Zero, and they made their way downtown, passing the elementary school and stepping around a couple of bicycles lying on their sides on the sidewalk. They didn't say much; Calvin deflected Zero's comments about soccer and the Yankees with one-word responses. He had a plan, and he was focusing on it the way he'd prepare for a basketball game or a race. Thinking. Going over the strategy in his head.

"I remembered something when I was cutting the lawn," he said finally as they reached St. Joseph's Church. "They got gymnastics at the Y this afternoon."

"Who does?"

"*Them.* Our new buddies."

"Oh."

"Should be coming out anytime now. Let's get a drink and hang."

They went into the market and wasted no time getting bottles of soda. Then they crossed back over the Boulevard and took a seat on the YMCA's cement front steps, watching traffic.

A bus went by after about ten minutes.

"One up," Zero said.

Calvin gave a short, huffy laugh. He stared at the message board on the Y's front lawn:

AEROBICS CLASSES NOW FORMING.
SUMMER DAY-CAMP OPENINGS.
MEN'S BASKETBALL SIGN-UPS.

"Hey, hey."

Danielle Rosado was standing in the doorway in a violet leotard and bare feet. She had athletic tape around her wrists, and her hands were white with chalk from the uneven bars. "What are you boys up to?" she asked.

"Hanging out," Zero said. "What are you doing?"

Danielle held up her hands and said, "Duh. Gymnastics."

"You good at it?" Zero asked.

Danielle shrugged. "I guess. Been doing it since I was five."

Calvin stood up. He was taller than Danielle, but he was standing three steps below her. So he climbed to the top step and pulled his shoulders back a little, trying to look built. He leaned on the railing.

"So," he said. "We play you guys on Tuesday."

"That right?"

"That's what the schedule says."

"Should be interesting."

"We think so."

Danielle looked back toward the gym. "Jessie's still on the bars."

Calvin took a gulp of his orange soda, then held

out the bottle to Danielle. "Want a hit?"

Danielle pulled back slightly and wrinkled her nose, then shook her head. "No thanks."

"Season's going fast," Calvin said. "Before you know it, we'll be in the playoffs."

"I guess."

"You know what? I think the church carnival is coming up already. That right, Z?"

"Yeah," Zero said. "I think it's next weekend."

"Next weekend?" Calvin said. "Wow. I didn't know that. You going to the carnival, Danielle?"

"Probably. We usually do."

"Yeah. Us, too."

Calvin inhaled deeply and let it out. "Hot day," he said.

"It's stifling in the gym," Danielle said. "That's why I came out here."

"Uh-huh," said Calvin. "Yeah." His throat felt very dry suddenly, so he took another swig of soda. "So . . . that carnival . . . you think you might be going, huh?"

Danielle looked amused. She raised her eyebrows and said, "Mm-hmm."

"Yeah . . . us, too."

"Maybe we'll see you boys there."

Calvin swallowed hard. "Yeah. Maybe Friday night?"

Danielle shrugged, but slowly. "Maybe."

"Me and Zero will probably get there around six."

Danielle smiled sweetly, but looked like she was holding back a giggle. "We probably will, too."

Calvin nodded about seven times. "That's a week from today. Six o'clock . . . we'll probably see you there. I guess."

Danielle wiped her hands together again. "I guess." She opened the door to go back into the gym. "See you at Tuesday's game. . . . Better practice hard."

8

Showdown

It was a perfect evening for soccer. Not too hot, not too humid. Hardly a breeze. Two unbeaten teams had completed half a game, and things stood even: Bauer Electric 0, Little Italy 0.

But the second half promised much more action. Danielle Rosado had spent the first half at goalie, and Jessie had played only part of the half. They'd be moving up to the front line for the rest of the game.

Across the field, Calvin was psyching himself up for a wild twenty-four minutes. He'd spent the first half at sweeper, keeping things clear at the defensive end but not having much impact on the offense. He'd be at midfield now, trying to control both ends of the field as he had in earlier games. Zero would be playing goalie. Things were looking favorable for Little Italy.

He looked upfield and saw Jessie at right wing staring across at him, her braids pulled back and held by a pink hair band. Danielle was at left wing, wearing a similar blue band. Between them at center was their cousin, Johnny Rodriguez.

Through three and a half games, no one had scored against Bauer Electric. Thinking over that fact gave Calvin a rush of energy. It was time to end the streak.

His chance came just minutes into the half. After Rodriguez sent a long line-drive shot directly into Zero's arms, Angel Medina fielded Zero's punt near midfield and darted along the sideline. Calvin went straight up the center of the field, staying level with Angel. Mary Pineda trailed behind Angel, providing an outlet for the ball when he got trapped by a couple of defenders.

Mary fielded the ball and crossed it over to Orlando Green at the left wing. Orlando dribbled forward, then sent the ball in front of Calvin, who raced toward it and one-touched it ahead, never breaking stride. His speed carried him past Danielle, and just one defender and the goalie stood between him and the net. Angel was streaking in from Calvin's right. Calvin gave him a leading pass, then moved around the defender, positioning himself for a return pass.

Calvin was just inside the goal box. Angel's crossing pass was perfectly placed. Calvin stepped quickly toward the ball, trapped it with his instep, and fired it into the goal.

He avoided celebrating as he jogged back for the kickoff, looking straight ahead and keeping his hands down. But he couldn't help himself as he got near Jessie, softly singing, "Un-de-*feat*-ed," as he ran past.

"Long way to go," she murmured. She spit on the ground and ran in place.

Jessie got the equalizer a few minutes later, taking a chip from the corner and stopping it cold with her foot, racing past Mary, and easily faking out Peter. Zero made a diving attempt at the shot, but the firmly hit ball slid under his fingertips and rippled the net.

Jessie returned the zinger to Calvin as she trotted up the field, singing, "In your *fa-a-a-a-ce,*" while Calvin shook his head and winced.

The teams battled frantically as the second half wound down. Calvin had one hard shot knocked down by the goalie, and Danielle came ever-so-close to sneaking one past Zero. But much of the action took place near the center of the field, with constant changes of possession and furious defensive efforts.

Two minutes were left when Bauer Electric made a charge down the field, with Johnny and Jessie doing most of the footwork. Calvin stayed between Jessie and the goal, determined that she wouldn't get off a clear shot.

Stop them here, Calvin thought. *We've got time for one big push down the other end.*

Danielle had the ball at the upper corner of the goal box, with Peter right on her. Danielle pivoted and crossed the ball to her sister, who took it at the top of the box, glaring at Calvin.

Jessie feinted left, then moved the ball to the right with the outside of her foot—the same move she'd faked Calvin out with at the preseason clinic. Calvin saw it coming and darted to that side, moving aggressively toward the ball.

And quicker than a bullet—much too quickly for Calvin to react—Jessie stepped on the ball to stop it, rolled it back to her left, and raced straight toward the goal. Calvin stumbled forward. Jessie booted the ball into the net. Bauer Electric led, 2–1.

Calvin regained his balance and stared at the sky in frustration. He felt a sharp jab in his bicep. "*Sssssss,*" said Danielle as she poked him with a finger. "You got burnt so bad you're steaming."

The seconds ticked away. Little Italy made one last run at the goal, but Johnny intercepted the ball for Bauer Electric and booted it long and hard down the field. The final whistle blew as Angel chased it down.

The spectators stood and clapped as the Bauer Electric players danced and leaped at midfield. Calvin and his teammates stood and stared, exhausted and beaten.

The teams met at midfield for congratulations. Calvin held back for a minute, then walked up to Jessie and shook her hand.

Jessie gave him a triumphant smile.

Calvin grimaced. "See you Friday?" he asked.

Jessie looked surprised. "Where at?"

"The carnival."

Her eyes got narrow. "Says who?"

"I don't know. Just thought we'd see you there. Me and Zero."

"Why'd you think that?"

Calvin let out his breath in a huff. "Danielle didn't say nothing?"

"Not about you turkeys." She looked around for her sister. "Danielle!"

Danielle was in the midst of a group of six or seven kids near the sideline. She jutted out her chin and called, "What's up?"

"Come over here, sister."

Danielle trotted over. Zero was walking over, too.

Jessie had her hands on her hips. "You know anything about a *carnival* situation, Danielle?"

Danielle smiled. "These boys might have said something. Wasn't exactly *definitive*."

Jessie squinted at Calvin and gave a tight half-smile. She reached forward and gripped the neck of his soaking T-shirt between her thumb and first finger. "You *got* anything definitive to say? Or to *ask*?"

Calvin squirmed and looked at the ground. Then he looked Jessie straight in the eye. "Yeah," he said firmly.

"So let's hear it." She let go of his shirt.

"Me and Zero just thought it might be cool to hang out with you two at the carnival. You know . . . just hang around. Go on rides and stuff."

Jessie looked at Danielle and flicked up her eyebrows. She was holding back a bigger smile. "What do you think, Danielle? These two worthy?"

Danielle broke into a very broad grin. "You know they're cute, Jessie." She turned to Calvin. "She's not as tough as she seems."

Jessie very gently kicked her sister in the shin. "So who'd be with who?" she said. "Or haven't you worked that out yet?"

Calvin shrugged.

"We may be twins, but we're not interchangeable dates," Jessie said. "Or should we do the choosing for you?"

Zero cleared his throat. "I think you should be with Calvin," he said to Jessie.

"Why? You afraid of me?"

"No." Zero took a step back. "Just think you and Calvin might be a better match."

"Works for me," said Danielle.

"You buy us dinner?" Jessie asked.

"Whatever," said Calvin.

Jessie glanced around the field, then kicked at the turf with her toe. "Okay," she said. "We'll give it a try. Six o'clock on Friday in front of the Y. Bring your wallets."

Both boys nodded vigorously. The girls walked away, laughing hard.

9

Half Sprite, Half Orange

Calvin banged on Zero's front door Friday at about five P.M., wearing a green polo shirt, neat black shorts with a belt, and a pair of running shoes with no socks.

"What'd you do?" Zero asked. "Raid your father's closet?"

"Real funny. What are *you* wearing?"

Zero had on the same brown shorts he'd been wearing all summer and a spotty T-shirt that said *Liberty State Park*. He looked down at the shirt. "What I'm wearing now?"

"No way."

"What's the difference?"

Calvin frowned and shook his head. He pointed toward the stairs. "Let's go."

Calvin opened Zero's bedroom closet and sifted through the shirts.

"I outgrew most of those this year," Zero said.

Calvin took out a blue-checked shirt with short sleeves and held it up. "This is okay," he said.

Zero shrugged and pulled off his T-shirt. "We ain't going to church," he said.

"It matters. Think *they'll* be wearing the same clothes they mow the lawn in?"

"Guess not."

They walked downtown, way early, and sat on the steps of the YMCA, watching traffic go by. The day was warm and dry. The carnival had opened at four, so plenty of kids they knew walked past, including their teammate Angel. Angel never said much at the games or practices. He was a year younger.

"Going to the carnival?" Zero asked.

Angel shook his head. "Maybe tomorrow," he said. "I gotta babysit for my little brother."

When the Rosados' station wagon pulled up a while later, Calvin felt a cold, empty rush in his stomach, and he swallowed hard. The twins and their father emerged from the car and walked toward them. Calvin stood up and yanked on Zero's shoulder until he stood, too.

Calvin's eyes were fixed on the father, who had a tight smile and was eyeing him back. He was wearing a starched white shirt and a blue tie, and his dark hair was neatly cropped.

"Shake his hand," Calvin said under his breath to Zero.

"Okay."

Zero stepped past the girls and stuck out his hand. "Hi, Mr. Rosado," he said.

"Hello, *Dr.* Rosado," Calvin said, giving Zero a hard, sidelong glance.

Dr. Rosado laughed. "Hello, fellas. Nice night for a carnival."

The boys nodded.

"You played a good game against my girls the other night."

"Yeah," said Calvin. "Hope we get a rematch in the playoffs."

Jessie was standing with one hand on her hip, looking them over. "Boys," she said in greeting.

"Hey, Jessie," said Calvin. "Hey, Danielle."

"So," Dr. Rosado said, rubbing his palms together. "Ferris wheel at ten o'clock, right? Or call if you need me earlier." He kissed both girls and winked at Calvin. "See you tonight."

"See ya," Calvin said. They stood on the sidewalk until Dr. Rosado had driven away.

Calvin gave Zero a hard nudge with his elbow. "He's a surgeon, stupid."

"How would I know?"

"Pay attention to the world."

"Oh, like you do?" Zero said sarcastically.

"I know things."

"You don't know everything."

Danielle and Jessie had started walking toward the carnival grounds, side by side. Calvin and Zero walked behind them until they got there.

The field was lined with dozens of booths featuring gaming wheels where you could win candy, stuffed animals, CDs, and T-shirts; food vendors with french fries, ice cream, steak sandwiches, and countless other items; coin tosses, basketball shoots, and face-painting; and lots more. On one end of the field were the Ferris wheel, merry-go-round, and other rides. Later there'd be a band.

"Too early to eat?" Calvin asked as he and Zero fell into step with the twins. The smells of sausages and pizza were making him hungry.

"Maybe we'll start with some fries," Jessie said. "Then move on to bigger things. What do you think, Danielle?"

"Fries sound good to me."

Both twins crossed their arms and gave the boys a look like, *We're waiting.* But they were smiling, too.

Zero and Calvin got in line at a fried-food stand. "This is gonna cost us," Calvin said.

"Yeah, they've got it all planned, I think." Zero opened his wallet and looked inside. "I got eighteen dollars."

"I got about thirty." Calvin looked back at the girls, who were talking to a couple of their friends. "We should be okay."

"They can't eat forty-eight bucks' worth of food."

"Nah. But we gotta eat, too. And pay for the rides."

"We'll stall," Zero said. "Always get on the longest lines."

Calvin nodded. "Right."

They walked over with the fries and joked around

a bit with Julie Carrasco, from their soccer team, and Sherry Allegretta, who they knew from track. When the fries were gone, Danielle said, "I could use a drink."

"Me, too," said Jessie. She raised her eyebrows and gave Calvin an expectant look.

"What do you want?" Calvin asked.

"Half Sprite, half orange. About this much ice only," Jessie said, holding her fingers about three-quarters of an inch apart. "With a straw."

Danielle shook her head and smiled gently at Zero. "A Coke will be fine," she said.

Calvin and Zero walked back to the same stand. They could hear the four girls giggling behind them.

When they were in line, Zero smacked Calvin's arm to get his attention. "Remember," he said, looking as serious as he could. "*This* much ice." Then he cracked up.

Calvin stuck his hands in his pockets and looked at the sky. "She's busting my chops, huh?"

"She's something else." Zero glanced over at the girls, who'd been joined by three guys their age—Vinnie DiMarco, Spencer Lewis, and Willie Shaw. "Why'd you pick *them,* anyway?"

"I don't know. They're cute, you gotta admit that. Jessie was a lot of fun last year in school. Always busting on the teachers and giving me gum and stuff."

"She likes being the center of attention," Zero said. "That's for sure."

"Maybe we can switch girls next time."

"Yeah, right. You think there's gonna *be* a next time?"

Calvin grimaced. "Who knows?"

"So what are we supposed to do? Follow them around all night and buy whatever they want?"

They'd reached the counter. Calvin hesitated, then said to the heavy guy in a red-and-white-striped shirt, "Can you give me half Sprite and half orange with just a little ice?"

"*This* much ice," Zero said, holding up his fingers, clearly enjoying himself while Calvin squirmed. "His date is a little fussy about that."

The guy smirked and nodded. "Aren't they all," he said. He went to get the drink.

"A Coke, too!" Zero called. "No special treatment needed."

Calvin elbowed Zero again, but he paid for both

drinks. The twins and their posse had walked over to one of the gaming booths, where Spencer was trying to win some candy by betting on a wheel. Spencer had been the starting point guard on the school basketball team and was considered one of the coolest kids in their grade. He was wearing a tank top that was stark white against his brown skin. He had muscular arms for a twelve-year-old.

After a few spins, Spencer won four chocolate bars. "For the ladies," he said, grinning broadly as he handed one each to Jessie, Danielle, Sherry, and Julie.

Calvin turned to Jessie. "Hope that don't spoil your appetite," he said with a touch of sarcasm.

"Don't worry," she replied. "I'm just warming up."

The group walked around the inner perimeter of the carnival grounds, stopping now and then to check out a booth or greet a friend. Zero and Calvin hung toward the back of the pack. Eventually Danielle joined them.

"How you guys doing?" she asked. She had a knowing grin.

Calvin shrugged. "Okay, I guess."

"My sister's a trip, huh? She knows how to get her way."

Calvin just nodded.

"You guys getting hungry for some real food?" Danielle asked.

"I am," Zero said. "I could go for a sausage sandwich."

"Sounds good." She gripped Zero's arm momentarily and pointed him toward an Italian food booth. "Catch you later," she said to Calvin.

Now Calvin found himself in a pack of seven people, with Jessie at the front and him trailing behind. She chattered away with Spencer and Sherry as they walked around the fair. After a couple of circuits, Calvin noticed Zero and Danielle waiting to get on the Ferris wheel.

Calvin caught up to Jessie and tapped her on the shoulder.

"Oh . . . hey, Calvin." She said it nicely, but acted like she'd been taken by surprise, as if he'd just arrived.

"You getting hungry?"

"Yeah. A little." She turned to Sherry. "What are you guys gonna do?"

Sherry shrugged. "Go on some rides, maybe."

"We'll see you later," Jessie said. She stopped

walking and looked at Calvin. "What do you feel like?"

"I don't know. Calzone or something?"

"Yeah. Something spicy."

They walked across the grounds. "Where's my sister?" Jessie asked.

"She and Zero took off a while ago. They hit some rides, I think."

They got calzones and onion rings and a wad of paper napkins and took a seat at a green plastic table under a big red tent.

"Thanks for buying the food," Jessie said. "I can pay for the rides."

"Cool. If you want."

Jessie still had her drink cup. She held it out to Calvin.

"No, thanks," he said. "I'll get something later."

"Okay."

"How was it, by the way?"

Jessie looked a little embarrassed as she smiled. "Just right." She took a sip, and the straw made a squishy sound as she reached the bottom of the cup. "Perfectly mixed."

Without an audience to show off for, Jessie had suddenly became a lot nicer. She asked Calvin how he liked soccer—"better than baseball, about even with football"—and reminded him of the day their math teacher had a big rip in the butt of his pants and didn't know it. He'd spent most of the class writing on the blackboard while the kids tried to hold back their laughter.

They found Zero and Danielle and went on the Tilt-A-Whirl and into the haunted house, then got ice-cream sandwiches and tried to win some CDs. They ended the night on the merry-go-round.

"That was great," Jessie said as they strolled through the crowd toward the Ferris wheel to wait for their father. "I'm definitely going back in the haunted house tomorrow."

"Tomorrow?" Calvin asked.

"Yeah." She took a seat on a bench. Zero and Danielle were lagging behind, having stopped to listen to a jazz trio that was playing near the center of the grounds. "Spencer asked me to come with him."

"*Spencer* did?"

"Yeah." Jessie looked around, a little embarrassed and a little bold. "When you were getting the soda earlier." She shrugged. "What the heck, right? The carnival's only once a year."

Calvin was quiet for a moment. "Did he know you were here with *me*?"

Jessie shrugged. "It wasn't very obvious, I guess. There were a lot of us hanging out by then."

Calvin stared at the ground. "Man," he said under his breath.

Jessie touched his arm, then drew her hand away. "It's not like this is a boyfriend thing," she said. Calvin wasn't sure if she meant him and Jessie, or Jessie and Spencer. Either way, there wasn't much to cheer about.

Jessie's tone brightened. "Anyway, I had a great time. Thanks for the food and everything."

"No problem."

Zero and Danielle had arrived, and Calvin could see Dr. Rosado walking toward them. "There's your dad," he said flatly.

"Yeah." Jessie stood up from the bench. "Thanks, guys," she said sweetly. "It was a blast."

"Thanks," said Danielle, giving them that little finger wave. "See you on the soccer field."

Calvin stood with his mouth hanging open as the girls walked away. Zero stared at him. "You okay?" he said.

Calvin shook his head slowly. "I guess," he said. "Man, that is one confusing girl."

"Confusing or confounding?"

"Both." Calvin started walking. "Never did get a drink tonight. I'm thirsty." He looked around the grounds. Spencer, Sherry, and the others were hanging with a large group over by one of the food tents. They were laughing and looking animated. "Let's get out of here," Calvin said.

He led the way out of the carnival grounds and down Ninth Street toward the Boulevard. "I had enough of this," he said.

"The grocery's closed," Zero said as they reached the main street. A few blocks up, the digital clock above the Hudson City National Bank said 10:09.

"I know a place," Calvin said. He was walking quickly. They were both supposed to be in by 10:30. "Might be a little late getting home, but we can weasel out of it."

Zero stayed in step with Calvin, who didn't say much as they walked past the mostly darkened stores. A few taverns and the pizza places were still open, and a Latin rhythm was coming from the Lupita Music store.

When they reached the corner of Third, Calvin said, "What's the count?" to the man with the German shepherd.

"One up, two down," was the reply.

"Must be a slow night," Zero said to Calvin.

"He just starts over when he gets to five."

"Where we going, anyway? It's getting late."

"Two more blocks," Calvin said. "We need to expand our horizons some, you know?"

They reached First Street, just inside the town's border, and Calvin turned down the hill toward the river. A quarter block down was Carolina's Cantina, a small Mexican restaurant that served mostly take-out food. There were just three tables, but there was a refrigerator stocked with juices and soda near the counter.

"How'd you know this would be open?" Zero asked.

"My dad knows every late-night place to eat around here," Calvin said. "We get tacos and stuff sometimes."

The round, dark-skinned man behind the counter nodded to the boys and smiled. He and two men at a table were watching a soccer game in Spanish on the small TV that was perched on a shelf next to cans of beans and tomatoes. Soccer posters on the wall said FUTBOL MEXICO and CLUB DE FUTBOL MONTERREY.

"That's our sport," Calvin said, pointing to the TV.

The men turned to him and grinned. "Who do you play for?" one asked. He had a strong Spanish accent.

"Little Italy. In the Y league."

The man behind the counter said, "We sponsor a team in the older division. You look like a striker."

Calvin shrugged. "They play me all over. It's my first year. . . ."

"You like it?"

"Bueno," Calvin said. Then he broke into an embarrassed grin. He didn't know much Spanish.

"Greatest sport in the world."

Calvin tapped on the glass door of the cooler at a row of sodas—Jarritos, Manzana, Lupiña—in mandarin orange, coconut, guava, pineapple. "*That* is good stuff," he said to Zero. "A whole lot better than mixing Sprite and orange-colored sugar water." He took out a bottle of pineapple soda. Zero reached in for another.

"We better hustle," Calvin said as they paid for the drinks. Then he had a second thought. He paid for a bottle of guava soda and held it up to the light. "For my dad. That'll make sure he gets over me being twenty minutes late."

Then they hurried out the door toward home.

10

Corner Kicks

Little Italy lost a close one to Hector's Garage but beat Bug Busters Extermination to run its record to 4–2–1. With three regular-season games remaining, they were in good position for a playoff spot.

The standings were taped to the wall of the refreshment stand at the recreation field. Calvin checked them out as he waited for the rematch with the Grotto.

EASTERN DIVISION	W	L	T
Little Italy	4	2	1
The Grotto	4	3	0

Luigi's	2	3	2
Villa Roma	1	6	0

WESTERN DIVISION	**W**	**L**	**T**
Bauer Electric	6	0	1
Hector's Garage	4	2	1
Bug Busters	2	4	1
H. C. Florist	1	4	2

Zero had gone into New York City with his parents and wasn't back yet when Calvin left for the match, so he'd walked over alone. Now, just ten minutes before game time, Zero still hadn't shown. Victor Alvarez was vacationing at Seaside Heights with his family, so Little Italy wouldn't have any substitutes if Zero didn't get there. The evening was hot and sticky.

"This is a big one," Coach Diaz said as the players gathered around him. He was wearing a yellow Brazil soccer jersey with green trim and had shaved off his wisp of a mustache. "If they beat us, we drop into second place. And whoever ends up second in our division is going to get Bauer Electric in the first round of the playoffs."

"We'll beat them," Calvin said, meaning Bauer Electric.

"They don't think so," said Coach, gesturing toward the Grotto players, who were warming up on the field. "They've been playing well the past few weeks. They want this rematch bad."

The Grotto was clearly fired up, and it showed in the opening minutes of the game. Mary Pineda was playing goalie for Little Italy and she made a couple of nice saves, but the third shot was unreachable and the Grotto had a quick 1–0 lead.

Calvin glanced over at the sideline and noticed that Zero had not yet arrived. "Let's suck it up," he called to his teammates. "Let's get it back."

The Grotto's three subs came running onto the field and took their spots on the front line. *This could be a problem*, Calvin thought. The opponents had the advantage of rotating their players frequently, getting fresh legs out there while the Little Italy players wilted in the heat.

And the pressure continued. Little Italy barely crossed midfield more than a couple of times, while the Grotto kept up a steady game of quick, short passes and runs at the goal. Calvin was ineffective from his position at sweeper, unable to help generate the offense. By halftime, the Grotto had a 2–0 lead.

Zero was standing near the bench as the players walked slowly off the field, needing drinks and rest. All seven players had been out there for the entire half.

"Where you been?" Calvin said sharply as he caught Zero's eye.

"Bad traffic at the tunnel," Zero said with a shrug.

"We're getting our butts kicked."

"We'll be all right."

Calvin moved closer to Zero and lowered his voice. "You better be ready to run with me, man. The rest of these people are out of gas."

Coach came over to them and said they'd be at the midfield positions in the second half. "You two have to control the game," he said. "We'll put Angel, Orlando, and Mary in the front line, but that'll leave our defense very vulnerable. We need to tie this game up, at least."

Calvin nodded. He went to the bench and grabbed his jug of water. His shirt was soaked with sweat. He shut his eyes and poured a bit of the water over his head.

"Different game this half," Coach said as the

players huddled up around him. "We put the pressure on now. We control the field."

It wasn't easy, but the mix of speedier players did make a difference for Little Italy. Calvin felt the frustration of having a long, sustained attack thwarted by an excellent save by the goalie, and he shook his head in resignation as the three rested Grotto players trotted onto the field soon after to give some teammates a breather.

The first break came when Orlando made a steal at midfield and found Mary looping over from the sideline with a world of space in front of her. She quickly covered twenty yards with the ball, then crossed it cleanly to Angel, who fielded it without breaking stride and hammered it high and hard into the net. Angel had become a consistently dangerous scorer.

"There we go!" Coach Diaz called, clapping his hands. "Plenty of time left. Keep it going."

Calvin crunched up the lower part of his shirt and wrung out a few drops of sweat. He looked over at Zero, who was staring intently toward the goal.

"Our turn," Calvin said. "The ice is broken."

Zero nodded. "I'm ready."

When Calvin intercepted a pass a few minutes

later, he dribbled two steps, then passed crisply to Zero. Mary was open on the wing again, and she darted across the center line and gave a quick juke, racing past a defender. She passed back to Angel who was trailing the play, and he chipped the ball ahead to Orlando.

Calvin was running nearly full-speed down the middle of the field, closing in on the goal box. Orlando's pass was shin-high and caromed off Calvin's leg, but Zero was in the right place and shot the bouncing ball toward the corner of the goal.

The Grotto goaltender dove hard, extending his hand and knocking the ball to the side. It cleared the goal but bounced off a defensive player's leg and over the end line.

"Corner kick!" called the official, and Orlando ran over to the corner flag to put the ball in play.

About three minutes remained in the game. Orlando's chip was high and soft. Calvin braced his forearm against an opponent's back, tensed and ready to leap for the ball, hoping to head it into the goal. But in the scramble for the ball he was shoved backward, and the goaltender safely caught the pass, ending the threat.

"No foul?" Calvin shouted. But the ball was already in play, so he raced back up the field.

The Grotto players were determined to preserve the one-goal margin, forgetting about offense and repeatedly clearing the ball with long, solid kicks.

"We have to pick them apart!" Calvin said urgently. "Control the ball. Short passes. Let's go!"

Peter Leung had come up from the sweeper position, giving an additional man to the Little Italy offense but leaving Julie unprotected back in goal. Only a minute was left as Peter came charging up the field one more time, chasing the ball as he ran.

Calvin knew that Peter's ball-control skills were barely adequate, so he ran over and shouted for the ball. Peter obliged. Calvin stopped the ball and looked up the field. Both teams were spread out before him. This might be the last run of the game.

"Support!" hollered Zero as Calvin was met near the center circle by a couple of opponents. Calvin passed back to Zero, then moved to an open space so Zero could return the ball.

Orlando was open, so Zero passed it there and ran. Orlando had room and he dribbled along the sideline. Calvin stayed level with him, with Zero trailing behind.

The pass went back to Zero, who found Angel darting across the top of the goal box. Angel pivoted and shot, a high line drive that the goalie leaped for, punching the ball over the top of the goal and out of bounds.

Another corner kick. The players bunched up in front of the goal, shoving for position. Calvin ran into the mix, then swerved around Zero and sprinted toward Orlando at the corner of the field.

Orlando saw him coming and changed tactics, making the short, easy pass instead of chipping it into the air in front of the goal. Two defenders charged toward Calvin, but he deftly dribbled around them and reached the goal box.

"Here!" came Mary's yell, and Calvin scooted the ball ten yards across the field, where his wide-open teammate fielded it and kicked it into the net. They'd tied it up!

Calvin, elated, ran toward Mary, grabbing her under the arms and lifting her into the air. Zero, Orlando, and Angel joined the embrace, shouting and raising their fists.

The official blew his whistle before the Grotto could put the ball in play. Game over. Little Italy was still in first place.

Calvin reached the sideline and yanked his T-shirt over his head, falling to the ground and lying on his back, his arms and legs spread wide. He was panting and sweating hard, but he'd never felt better. His teammates were re-energized, slapping hands and grinning in the wake of their spectacular comeback.

Suddenly Calvin felt a stream of cool liquid on his forehead and he opened his eyes and sat up. Danielle Rosado was standing there, holding a bottle of water and laughing. "Looked like you needed some cooling off," she said.

"At least I'm not sizzling this time," Calvin said with a smile.

"We brought you guys something."

"Oh yeah?" Calvin got to his feet. Jessie was there, too, holding a paper plate covered with foil.

"Made some cookies for you and Zero," Jessie said.

"How come?"

Jessie shrugged. "You know. . . . A thanks for the carnival."

"Yeah." Calvin took the plate and peeked under the foil. "Chocolate chip. Beautiful."

Calvin looked at Jessie now—black soccer shirt, pink hair band, mischievous smile. "Thanks," he said. "These won't last long."

Jessie nodded. "Gotta warm up now."

"Who you playing?"

"The flower shop. Shouldn't be a problem."

"Maybe we'll watch," Calvin said. "And eat our cookies."

"You better watch," Jessie said. "Could be you and us in the finals, you know. . . . I think you guys still need some education."

"Maybe so," Calvin answered. "But we did the educating tonight. We shut those guys down and came back."

Jessie nodded as she trotted onto the field. "Not bad," she said, looking back. "Not bad at all."

11

The Playoffs

"Good job on the lawn," Mr. Tait said as Calvin came in for lunch.

Calvin just nodded. He'd been in a sour mood all morning, edgy about that night's game. Besides, the mower did the work; all he did was push it around.

Mr. Tait opened the refrigerator and took out a carton of orange juice. "Big one tonight, huh?"

Calvin felt a chill in his gut. He'd been trying not to think about it.

Wins over Luigi's and Villa Roma had clinched the division title for Little Italy and set them up for a first-round playoff game against Hector's Garage. They'd lost the regular season match to Hector's, 3–2.

"Those guys are fast," Calvin said. He blew out his breath. "It's do or die tonight. Playoffs."

Mr. Tait looked at his nails, which were perfectly trimmed and clean. "Nobody faster than you, from what I've seen." The Taits had only been to a couple of games, but Calvin had played well both times.

Calvin stared at the chicken sandwich on his plate. He didn't feel very hungry. "I'm just one guy."

"You've got some good players." Mr. Tait took a seat and looked closely at his son. "The pressure is always worse before a playoff game," he said. "The intensity's higher. And an athlete *always* thinks he's going to blow it in the hours before a big match. The good ones simply keep focusing more and more intently as the game gets closer. Visualizing success. By game time, you're in such a strong emotional zone that nothing can break through and deter you."

Calvin looked his dad in the eyes and nodded. He'd been through things like that before, especially at track meets when the entire burden of winning or losing was on him. Dad was right—he had team-mates to share the load with tonight. There was some comfort in that.

"Think positive thoughts, and I guarantee you'll

have your best game ever," Mr. Tait said. "You're primed for this. You've been working for it all summer."

"That's true."

"And eat. I know how you're feeling—like that sandwich is going to sit in your stomach all day like a rock—but you need fuel."

Calvin took a bite and chewed about a hundred times. Then he swallowed hard. He set the sandwich on the plate and stared at it.

Six more hours until game time.

Calvin and Zero tried to make the afternoon go quickly, but it dragged. They went to the middle school and shot baskets on the blacktop court, playing a few games of O-U-T instead of going one-on-one, which would have drained too much energy.

Then they went down to the high school, crossing the parking lot and through an opening in the chain-link fence behind the football field and the track. There was a thick cluster of trees beyond the fence for about twenty yards, then a steep, sudden drop. The cliffs.

The cliffs ran for much of the length of Hudson

City, dropping at a sharp angle to the flat area along the Hudson River. Only four streets ran down to the flats—First and Sixteenth at the opposite ends of town, and Franklin and Ninth, more or less at either end of Hamilton Park along the river.

From this point above the cliff, the boys had a clear view across to New York City. The cliffs weren't steep enough to be dangerous, but most of the mile-long stretch was undeveloped—just trees and boulders and narrow paths. It was a good place to while away an hour or so, watching the boats on the river and the traffic on Palisades Avenue running from Jersey City to Hoboken. It was a bit of an oasis amid the glass and steel and concrete of one of the world's busiest metropolitan areas.

"We gotta get the jump on those guys tonight," Calvin said, tossing a stick down the hill at a rock several feet away. He missed. "We always seem to be falling behind to good teams and then scrambling our way back. Would be nice to get an early lead for a change."

Zero kept looking at the river. Then he turned toward Calvin in a hurry and said, "What?"

"Nothing."

"I wasn't listening."

"I know. I said we need to start fast."

"When?"

"*Tonight.* In the game."

"Oh."

Calvin leaned back against a tree. All he could think about was the game. Seemed like Zero hadn't given it a second thought.

"Don't worry so much," Zero said. "We'll rise to the occasion. We always do."

"Do we?"

"Usually."

Calvin picked up a pebble and fired at the rock again. This time he hit it, and the pebble bounded down the hill.

"Nice shot," Zero said, with just a touch of sarcasm.

Calvin frowned. He had a lot of energy to burn. He needed to keep it in check until tonight.

They arrived at halftime of the first playoff game. Bauer Electric had a 2–0 lead over the Grotto and appeared to be comfortably headed for the finals. A big, noisy crowd was on hand to watch, filling the small bleachers and lined up along the sidelines.

Calvin hadn't eaten dinner. All he'd ingested since that chicken sandwich at lunchtime had been a nectarine and a glass of orange juice. There was a light breeze and the heat had eased off a bit. The temperature was in the low eighties.

Zero and Calvin set their cleats and their game shirts on the lowest step of the bleachers and walked to the sideline to watch the second half.

The Grotto scored a goal and seemed to steal the momentum for a few minutes. But then Danielle Rosado made a breathtaking series of fakes and found her cousin Johnny wide open for a goal that quickly deflated their opponents. Jessie scored again a few minutes later.

By then, the Hector's Garage players were doing some warm-up drills on the grass near the refreshment stand, decked out in lime green jerseys and shouting in Spanish and English.

Calvin looked around for his teammates. Peter and Julie were talking in the bleachers, not even watching the game. Angel and Orlando were stretched out on the grass, looking at the sky.

"Think they're ready?" Calvin said to Zero.

"Everybody gets ready in their own way," Zero said. He looked around and chewed on his lower lip. "Maybe we better take charge, though."

So they got the team together and passed a ball around until the coach arrived.

First half. Calvin started at sweeper and Zero at midfield. Coach had said before the game that he wanted Zero in the action all night instead of at goaltender.

Hector's had a couple of short, quick forwards who were skilled dribblers and played a possession style of soccer, patiently moving the ball around and occasionally making an assault on the goal.

Calvin's early jitters turned to confidence as Little Italy repeatedly thwarted Hector's offensive drives. Most of the play was near the middle of the field. The half ended without any scoring.

Trotting off the field, Calvin nodded toward his parents and little sister, who were standing in the bleachers and clapping. He took a seat on the bench and drank some water. So far, so good.

"Midfield," Coach said, pointing to Calvin. "Take control."

"Got it," Calvin said. That had been his second-half role all season. He'd have Angel alongside him, with Zero, Mary, and Orlando on the front line.

Calvin tapped Angel on the shoulder. The younger player looked up at him, eyes wide.

"Let's kick butt," Calvin said. He knew Angel could run all day, like he could. Calvin respected that.

Second half. Both teams still looked cautious, studying the situation, hoping for a quick opening that could break the tie, but also unwilling to take a risk that could give the other team an advantage.

Calvin knew this was the type of game where one great athletic play—the kind he was capable of—could make all the difference. He kept looking for that chance, but the opponents' defense was solid.

By the midpoint of the half, Calvin's frustration was growing. *Need to tire them out,* he thought. He fielded a pass from Angel and shouted, "Let's move!"

He dribbled hard, darting across the center line and cutting toward the sideline. Two defenders hustled over and had him trapped.

Zero yelled, "Support!" from behind, but Calvin booted the ball way up the field and kept chasing it.

A defensive player trapped the ball and chipped it ahead. Calvin kept running toward the ball, and he and Orlando converged on the midfielder who had it. That player quickly passed to one of those short, quick forwards, who dribbled rapidly along the sideline, heading for Little Italy territory.

Calvin's teammates had caught on and began swarming toward the ball, moving with greater energy and intensity. It seemed like every time an opponent got the ball, there were two Little Italy players in his face. Long runs, quick passes, and increased hustle led to shots on goal by Zero and Mary. But as the clock wound down, the game remained scoreless.

"Two minutes," said the official as Orlando took the ball near midfield for a throw-in.

Orlando stepped forward and made a mighty heave toward Angel. Angel came up and met the ball, sliding it across the top of the goal box. Calvin was there, sprinting in and shielding the ball from a defender.

There was no clear shot, but time was running out. Calvin planted his right foot and shot awkwardly with his left, sending the ball on a soft line drive toward the center of the goal. The goalie scrambled over, ready to make the easy save, but seemingly out of nowhere a defender stepped in front, heading the ball toward the corner of the field.

It looked like a heroic play, but unfortunately for Hector's, it backfired. Orlando was there, chipping the ball back in front of the goal. Angel lunged for it, catching it squarely with his forehead and knocking it across the goal line and into the net. The Little Italy players leaped and yelled as their opponents stared in disbelief.

Angel shook his fists and dropped to his knees, shouting, "Yes!" as his teammates surrounded him.

"Keep it up!" Calvin shouted. "Everything we've got now. Intensity!"

The final minute ticked away as Hector's frantically tried to even the score. Zero made a steal. The whistle blew. Little Italy was going to the final.

Calvin raised both arms toward the sky and let out a furious breath. He wanted that title. Now it was within his grasp.

12

Pineapple Soda

"Tomorrow night," Coach Diaz said as his jubilant team gathered around him. "Game time is seven o'clock. Be here by six fifteen."

"Championship game," said Angel, who'd been soaked with water by his teammates after scoring the winning goal.

"We had two losses all season, and we avenged the first one tonight," Coach said. "Now get a good rest and be ready to make amends for the second one."

Calvin put his hand on Angel's shoulder as they walked off. "You made the difference," he said.

Angel shrugged. "Just was in the right place at the right time," he said. "Orlando made the play."

"Wasn't just that," Calvin said. "You've been getting better every game."

"We all have."

Calvin's parents and sister had walked over.

"Okay if me and Zero hang out awhile?" Calvin asked.

"I suppose," Mr. Tait said. "Thought you might want to go out and celebrate with us."

Calvin peeled off his T-shirt as his mom handed him a dry one. "No reason to celebrate yet," he said. "How about tomorrow night?"

"Win or lose?" said his mom.

Calvin nodded. "Yeah, but we're going to win."

"Be in by ten," Mrs. Tait said. "Stay on the Boulevard."

"We will."

Zero and Calvin started walking across the field.

"Where we going?" Zero asked.

"I don't know. Get some food. Whatever."

A car's beep from the parking lot made them turn and look. The Rosados' station wagon was pulling out. Jessie had the front window open and was pointing at them with a big grin. "You're going down tomorrow night!" she shouted playfully.

Calvin put up his hands and staggered backward. "I'm shaking!" he yelled back.

Jessie just waved as the car pulled out of the lot.

They walked up to the market and bought packages of Yodels.

"You ain't thirsty?" Zero asked.

"Yeah, but I want one of them pineapple sodas. You up for walking?"

"Sounds good."

The sun had gone down but the evening was still light. It wasn't quite eight thirty, so they had plenty of time to kill.

"Think we can beat them?" Zero asked.

"Yeah. We can."

They walked past the bank and Izabella Bridal and the Habana restaurant, then took a seat on a bus-stop bench just outside Villa Roma to eat their Yodels. From there they could listen to the music coming from the pizza place, which had its doors wide open. The music was mostly from the 1970s and '80s—the Rolling Stones, Madonna, Aerosmith.

"Let's get that soda," Calvin said around nine, and they walked toward the south end of town.

When they reached Fourth Street, Zero looked ahead a block and said, "There he is."

"Who?"

"The Count."

Calvin stopped walking and thought for a second. "Let's go slow," he said. "Don't startle him."

"Why not?"

"Maybe we can get him to talk."

Zero let out a short laugh. "You mean more than what's up and down?"

"Yeah."

"I don't think there's much going on in his head besides that," Zero said.

"You never know." Calvin started walking again. "But my dad says he's never talked to nobody."

They walked up to the bench. "Hey," Calvin said, as friendly as he could.

The Count turned to the boys and caught Calvin's eye. He didn't smile but he didn't sneer. He jerked his gaze back toward the street. "Three up, one down," he said quickly. The German shepherd moved a little closer to him, looking up at the boys, but wagging his tail.

"That's a good score," Calvin said, taking a seat

on the edge of the bench. Zero stood behind him, on the side of the bench farthest from the Count.

"Good score," Calvin said again. "Mind if we watch for a while?"

The Count glanced at Calvin, then turned the other way and looked down the Boulevard toward Jersey City. He turned slowly back and said, "Three . . . three . . . three up. One down."

"I'll remember that."

Zero squeezed onto the bench and Calvin slid over, a little closer to where the Count was standing. The dog whined but kept wagging its tail.

"Nice night," Calvin said. "Beautiful night to be counting buses."

The Count kept his eyes on the road, scanning up the street and down. They were all quiet for about five minutes. Then the dog stiffened and faced back in the direction the boys had come, letting out a soft *woof*.

"Good dog," Calvin said as a bus came down the Boulevard. "Three up, two down," he said aloud. "Could be an unbelievable comeback for the downers."

The Count turned to Calvin and nodded quickly,

but his facial expression remained the same. "Three up, two down," he said, more to himself than to Calvin.

Another bus came down the street just a few minutes later, tying the score. Calvin stood up. "Can we pet your dog?" he asked.

The dog answered for him, pulling back his ears and growling. Calvin stepped away and said, "No problemo."

They made a wide path around the dog and began walking toward First Street again. "We'll be back," Calvin said to the Count. The Count did not acknowledge them.

They walked a block in silence.

"Pretty weird," Zero finally said.

Calvin let out a low whistle. "You got that right."

Carolina's Cantina was full of people. All the tables were full and several men were leaning against the counter, watching a soccer game on the little TV. The round man who ran the place at night recognized Zero and Calvin and smiled as they came in. "Hola," he called.

"Hola," Calvin answered. "Big game?"

"Barcelona," the man said. "Big game."

"Us, too," Calvin said. "Won our playoff game tonight. Championship game tomorrow."

"Bueno," came the answer. "Excellent."

"Mucho," Calvin said. "Big thirst."

The man grinned. Calvin grabbed a pineapple soda. Zero decided to try mandarin orange.

"Get two of those," Calvin said.

"One for your dad?"

"Nah. Got an idea."

They paid for the drinks. The man at the counter said, "Good luck tomorrow."

"Gracias," Calvin replied, using one of the last Spanish words he knew.

They walked back up to the Boulevard and over to Third Street, where the Count and his dog still stood.

"Four up, four down," the Count said without even being asked.

"Pretty exciting," Calvin said. He stood behind the bench. "Got sodas. Got one for you."

The Count took a quick glance at Calvin, then resumed looking up and down the Boulevard for buses.

"Want it?" Calvin said, holding up the extra bottle.

The Count did not look over.

"It's really good," Calvin said. He took a long swallow from his own bottle. He set the unopened one on the bench. "I'll just put this here in case you want it. It's not open. We didn't spit in it or anything like that."

They all watched the road for a few minutes. Then the dog stiffened and let out another *woof* as a bus came up the hill from Jersey City.

"That clinches it," Calvin said.

The Count nodded. "Five up, four down," he said.

Calvin turned to Zero. "Guess we should get going."

"Guess so," said Zero. "Just leave the bottle for him?"

Calvin shrugged. "Yeah. Maybe he'll drink it if we leave." He drummed on the top of the bench for a few seconds, then said, "Have a good night, my man. You too, doggy. We gotta get some sleep. Tomorrow evening we'll be counting *goals.*"

13

Overtime?

The biggest crowd of the season was on its feet, applauding the move Calvin had made. With time ticking down toward the end of the first half, he'd raced all the way up from his sweeper position to add some offensive pressure when Orlando set up a corner kick. Orlando had lofted the ball right in front of the goal, and Calvin sneaked into the chaos, stole the ball from Johnny Rodriguez, and fired it into the net, tying the score.

"One up, one down!" called Zero as Calvin came back to the defensive end.

Calvin grinned. Bauer Electric had controlled the action for most of the half, but had managed just one goal. It was anybody's game now. Either team could win the championship.

The whistle blew a minute later and the Little Italy players ran to the sideline, shaking their fists and whooping. All season long they'd been a second-half team. They could already feel the shift in momentum.

"We *own* the second half," Coach Diaz said. "Zero, Orlando, and Mary up front. Angel and Calvin at midfield."

Calvin put his hand on top of Angel's bristly head. "Let's go, little man. Constant pressure."

Angel nodded. "We'll shut them down," he said. "They won't get by us."

Calvin walked to the bench and took a seat next to Zero. "Ready to run?"

"All day," Zero said. He'd played goalie in the first half, so his legs were fresh. Everything was looking good.

Of course, Bauer Electric put all of its strength up front, too, with Danielle and Jessie at the wings and Johnny at center. The girls were looking across at Calvin with twin expressions of amusement.

"You're the best player on the field," Zero said

quietly as they walked out for the second half. "Remember that."

Calvin frowned. He didn't think that was true, but even if it was, Bauer Electric had three great players on the front line.

The Bauer Electric strategy was clear right from the kickoff—pound that ball toward the Little Italy goal, run like crazy, and keep continual pressure with passes and shots.

Little Italy staved off the bombardment for several minutes, finally getting some breathing room when Julie cleared the ball with a booming kick and Angel chased it down. Jessie and Danielle put on a burst of speed to catch him as a Bauer Electric defender met him from the other side. The ball was booted out of bounds.

"Throw in, orange," called the referee. Angel grabbed the ball at the sideline and looked around.

"Here," shouted Calvin, who was open in the backfield. Angel made the throw and Calvin scanned the field.

All of the Bauer Electric players had hustled back on defense, so that end of the field was crowded. They were obviously ready to run—getting everybody up when they had the ball, then everybody back on defense.

"Gotta pick 'em apart!" Calvin yelled, making a short pass to Zero. He ran across the center line, searching for an open space.

The Bauer Electric defense seemed impenetrable. It would take all the skill Calvin's teammates had just to get down near the goal. And as soon as Danielle, Jessie, or Johnny got the ball, the pressure was on again.

Here was Jessie, dribbling along the sideline, looking ahead to where two other black shirts were drifting in toward the goal. Calvin darted over to slow her down. She threw in a series of familiar moves.

Watch the ball, Calvin remembered. He moved closer and nudged the ball out of Jessie's grasp, kicking it out of bounds.

Jessie turned her head as Calvin backed away. "Lucky," she said with a grin.

Calvin shook his head. "No," he said, not smiling. "I'm on to you."

Jessie threw the ball in to Danielle, who had sneaked down the sideline, about ten yards in from the corner flag. She had an open path to the goal, and Zero and Julie came rushing over to slow her down.

Calvin's instinct was to stop Danielle, but he knew better than to have three defenders on one player. *Stick with Jessie*, he told himself.

Danielle stopped short, pushed the ball to her left with the outside of her foot, and darted past Zero, who stumbled toward the end line. Zero caught his balance and lunged back toward Danielle, colliding instead with Julie, who'd been tricked by another move.

Peter, in as goaltender for Little Italy, rushed over to the post, trying to cut off Danielle's angle. But she was moving fast, and Calvin saw that she would probably get off a shot. He took three quick steps toward her. He'd get to the ball before she could shoot.

But Danielle didn't shoot. She deftly brought her right foot to the top of the ball, pulling it away from Calvin's charge, and slid it across the goal mouth ahead of her sister.

It was no contest. Jessie took the pass and drove it into the wide-open goal. Peter hadn't even had a chance to move away from the post.

Calvin smacked his fist into his palm. He'd left Jessie alone. Peter would have made that save if Danielle had taken the shot. "My fault," he said.

Peter let out his breath and looked at the sky. "Mine, too," he said. "Get it back. Tie this thing up."

Calvin looked at the bleachers, then ahead to his opponents. Jessie had a huge grin and was slapping hands with her cousin. Calvin had to take over now.

"How much time?" he asked the official.

"Almost four minutes."

Enough time to at least tie the game and send it into overtime. Calvin took a deep breath. Make the plays, run like a cheetah. Utilize his teammates but take over the game.

Zero kicked off and Orlando fielded it as Calvin ran full speed toward the Bauer Electric goal. He looped back toward the sideline, yelling for the ball and taking a long pass from Angel. He passed back to Zero and ran hard toward the goal again.

Mary had the ball now, directly in front of the goal but thirty yards away. Calvin darted toward her. "Right here," he shouted.

The pass arrived. Calvin put his head down and charged forward. Jessie was in his path. Calvin stepped left, then took the ball to his right. He was too far from the goal but he shot anyway—a low, hard line drive that had a chance. The goalie dove for the ball and caught it, rolling to his feet and looking upfield.

"That's *my* move," Jessie said as she and Calvin ran side by side toward the corner.

Calvin was puffing hard. The pass came to Jessie. She shielded it from Calvin as she ran up the sideline, swerving left, then right, keeping him guessing.

As they approached the center line, Calvin stepped in front of her, knowing that would force her toward the middle of the field. He'd seen Zero shifting over to help out.

As he expected, Jessie moved to her right, then stopped the ball as she saw Zero approaching fast. Calvin had timed it perfectly, slipping his left foot to the ball, knocking it between Jessie's legs, and leaving her flat-footed as he sprinted away with it.

The field was wide open—forty yards of grass between him and the goalie. He booted it ahead and chased it down, eating up ground in a hurry, looking at the goalie who was the only thing standing between Calvin and a tied-up game.

He could hear the cheers from the bleachers, and Coach Diaz shouting, "All the way, Calvin!" He could hear Jessie's footsteps behind him.

A few more strides and he was close enough to shoot. He could see the fear in the goalie's eyes, sense the tension as he crouched, ready to spring toward the ball when Calvin finally shot.

Now! Calvin was inside the goal box, the defense was closing in from behind. With all the power he had, Calvin booted the ball high and hard. The goalie leaped.

Thunk! The ball bounded off the crossbar and back onto the field. Calvin's momentum kept him stumbling toward the goal. By the time he'd caught himself, the ball was in Johnny's possession, halfway up the field and moving quickly away.

Calvin had nothing left but he raced straight toward the ball. The Little Italy defense slowed down the charge, but Danielle had the ball near the goal box by the time Calvin had run up.

A quick pass to Jessie. A juke, a shot, another goal.

Calvin sunk to his knees and put his hands on the grass. His arms were shaking and his chest was heaving. He stared at the ground.

Orlando and Zero pulled him to his feet. The Bauer Electric players were locked in a huge embrace near midfield.

"One minute left," the official said.

Calvin felt a tap on his shoulder. He turned to see Victor Alvarez.

"I'm in for you," Victor said.

Calvin nodded and trotted off the field. There was some clapping as he reached the sideline. Coach Diaz put his arm around him and squeezed. "Great job," Coach said. "Great job all season."

Calvin dropped to his knees again and stared at the field for the final minute. He watched as the Bauer Electric players danced and leaped after the whistle. His teammates walked dejectedly off the field.

"We got thrashed," Calvin said as he caught up to Zero.

"We were in it until the final minute," Zero said. "That's no thrashing. We could have won it."

The teams met at midfield to shake hands. Jessie gave Calvin the warmest smile she'd ever managed. "You were awesome," she said.

"You, too."

"Tough break hitting that crossbar."

Calvin shook his head gently. "Got too far under the ball," he said. "Gotta learn how to shoot."

"I'll help you," she said. "It's not so hard if you practice."

Calvin smiled for the first time in a while.

Danielle squeezed Calvin's arm. "You all right?" she asked. "Thought you were gonna collapse out there."

Calvin rolled his eyes and nodded.

"You were tough," Danielle said. "That game could have gone either way."

Yes, it could have, Calvin thought. That's what he loved about sports. If you made the effort, gave everything you had, then at least you'd be in a position to win. You wouldn't always come out ahead, but you wouldn't always be on the losing end, either.

He held his head higher as he walked off the field. His parents were smiling and clapping for him. Coach Diaz was shaking hands with Dr. Rosado, and Angel and Orlando were laughing as they squirted water at each other from their drink bottles.

Zero came up and punched Calvin lightly on the shoulder. "Three down, one up," he said.

Calvin took off his jersey and wiped his face.

They'd lost. There wasn't much to say about it. But there were lots of seasons ahead. Basketball, baseball, track. Football practice would start in less than a week.

There were plenty of chances to come out a winner. Plenty more chances to even the score.

* * *

READ AN EXCERPT FROM

EMERGENCY QUARTERBACK:

WINNING SEASON #5!

Jason lined up in the shotgun. He took the snap and drifted toward Calvin's side of the field, watching for just the right second to unload the pass. But Anthony was already in pursuit, and line-backer Anderson Otero was circling toward him as well. Calvin was tightly covered. This wasn't going to work.

Jason pivoted and ran wide around Anthony, scrambling toward the other side of the field. He was twelve yards behind the line of scrimmage, in danger of a huge loss if he was caught. But his speed carried him past the on-rushing linemen, and suddenly he was heading up field, going wide around the end and cutting along the sideline.

The field was clear ahead of him, but Willie Shaw was racing over from his cornerback position, and the angle between them was to Willie's advantage. Jason upped his speed another notch, tucking in the ball and sprinting. Willie dove and Jason leaped, feeling Willie's hand slip off his calf. Jason landed hard, caught his balance, and ran unchallenged into the end zone.

Jason trotted back. Coach had called all of the players together, and they were standing near him or kneeling with their helmets off.

"That's what I was looking for," Coach said. "Without Vinnie in there, we need to adjust in a big way. Jason hasn't got the experience, but he's certainly got the athleticism."

"You've got to be kidding me!" came Wade's voice. Everyone turned to look at him.

"*I'm* the quarterback," Wade said. "You said he was just the emergency guy."

"That's right," Coach replied.

"Sounds like you're planning to switch to him."

"I haven't made that decision yet," Coach said. "But Jason's got the talent we need. Your status hasn't changed, Wade. We need you. But we need to explore all the options. We've got a championship to win."

* * *